Message from the Stars

Story by George Ivanoff
Illustrations by Alessandro D'urso

Contents

Chapter 1

Nothing Is Right

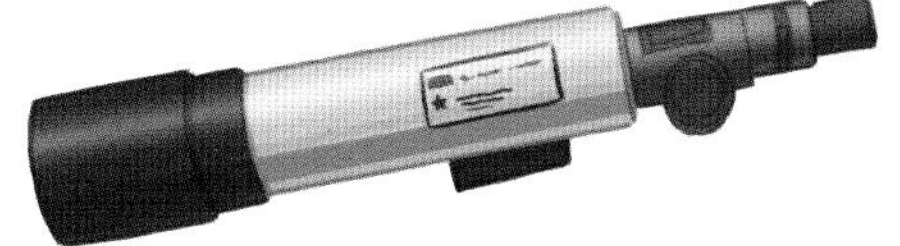

Aliens! Sirius loved thinking about the possibility of alien life, and he loved staring up at the stars through Dad's telescope. In fact, that's what he and Dad should have been doing right now.

But they weren't. They couldn't, because Dad wasn't there with Sirius. Dad was on the other side of the world.

So, Sirius was trying to talk with Dad on the computer instead. But the picture kept freezing and breaking up. The sound kept stopping and starting. It was making it very difficult to have a conversation.

"I really miss you, Sirius," said Dad. "And I know that you miss me, too."

Sirius just nodded. He was trying his best not to cry, and he was worried that if he said anything, he might not be able to stop the tears.

"Your mum tells me that you've been a bit upset ever since I left," Dad continued.

Sirius shrugged.

The screen froze for a few seconds, distorting the image of his dad. When it returned to normal, his dad was halfway through a sentence.

"... to worry. You can't let my absence stop you from doing all the things you normally do."

Sirius didn't respond.

"I'd really like it if you tried to carry on as usual." Dad paused and gave him a half-smile. "Could you do that for me?"

"Maybe," said Sirius. He shrugged again.

Dad started to say something else, but the screen froze. After a few seconds, it went black, the connection lost.

As Sirius switched off the computer, he could feel tears beginning to well up.

Chapter 2

Astronomy

Sirius's mum found him sitting in front of the black computer screen.

"How did the video call go?" she asked.

Sirius didn't answer. He didn't even turn around.

His mum gently swivelled his chair around, and saw that he'd been crying.

"Oh, honey." She enveloped him in a hug. "I miss him, too."

"It's not fair," said Sirius.

"I know it seems that way," his mum said, letting go of him and pulling up another chair. "But this is your dad's dream job. And it's only for one year."

"That's ages!"

"You can talk to him every day on the computer," she said.

"It's not the same," whispered Sirius. "And the computer keeps freezing."

"Well, that's something that I can fix." Mum smiled.

Sirius looked up, curious.

"I'm going to upgrade our internet service," said Mum. "It should make having conversations with Dad a lot easier. And it will all hopefully be in place by the time you get home from school tomorrow."

“I don’t want to go to school,” said Sirius.

“Sirius, we’ve been through this already,” said Mum. “You had a day off to go to the airport to say goodbye on Thursday, and I let you stay home on Friday as well. You’ve had the weekend to get used to things, and you’ve had the chance to speak with your dad this evening. So, tomorrow, it’s back to school. Even though Dad’s not here, we need to get back to life as usual.” She looked at him. “Okay?”

Sirius shrugged.

Mum got up to leave, but stopped at the door. She turned to Sirius. "I know it's late already, but …" She smiled. "If you want, you can bring your dad's telescope outside and set it up on the back deck for half an hour."

Sirius looked over at the telescope standing in the corner of the room. He and Dad had spent hours in the backyard using it to look up at the stars. But tonight, Sirius couldn't bring himself to do it on his own.

Dad was an astronomer – a scientist who studied space. That's why Sirius had been named "Sirius". As well as being his name, it was also the name of the brightest star in the sky. Well, actually, this star was made of two stars that orbited each other, so it was known as a binary star. But in the night sky, it appeared as just one bright point of light. Dad taught Sirius how to find his star in the sky.

When Sirius was younger, Dad would call him "my bright little Star-boy". Sirius allowed himself a half-smile as he remembered.

For all of Sirius's life, Dad had worked at the local university. But all of a sudden, he had been offered a new position – a chance to work on an astronomy project at one of the world's largest radio telescopes. That radio telescope happened to be at the Green Bank Observatory in West Virginia. And West Virginia was in the USA. It was a long way away.

Sirius left the telescope where it was and got himself ready for bed.

Chapter 3

Distracted at School

"Sirius? Hello, Sirius? Are you okay?"

Sirius jumped, suddenly realising that he hadn't been paying attention. Ms Whitford, his teacher, was standing right in front of him. The other kids were already out of their seats and heading out of the classroom.

"What?" Sirius asked.

"The bell has gone," said Ms Whitford. "It's lunch-time."

"Oh."

"Are you okay, Sirius?" she asked again. There was a look of concern in her eyes. "You've been a bit distracted all morning."

"I'm fine," he said, packing up his stuff.

"All right," said his teacher slowly, but she didn't look convinced. "Maybe some lunch will perk you up."

Sirius nodded, then headed for his school bag. He fished out his lunch box and went outside. The sun was shining, and a pleasant breeze stirred the leaves on the trees. He looked around, seeing his two best friends, Nirav and Keiko, sitting on a bench under a jacaranda tree. They were comparing lunches to see if there was anything they wanted to swap. They did this every day.

Normally, Sirius would be with them. But today, he wanted to be alone.

He set off quickly along the side of the school. There were some bushes at the end of the path, and a small patch of grass behind them. It was a hidden spot – a place he could go to be alone.

"Hey, Sirius!" he heard Nirav calling.

Sirius pretended not to hear as he slipped through the bushes and out of sight.

Chapter 4

A Mysterious Package

When Sirius returned home from school, he was still feeling miserable. He couldn't remember anything that Ms Whitford had said in class, and he had barely spoken to his friends. He felt really lonely. He was ready to crawl into bed and ignore the world. But he didn't get the chance.

The moment Sirius walked through the front door, Mum was rushing towards him excitedly.

"You've got a package," she announced.

"What sort of a package?" Sirius asked.

"A really big one!" She grabbed his hand and rushed him to his room.

The package *was* big. It was almost as tall as Sirius.

"What is it?" he asked.

"I have no idea," answered Mum.

"Who's it from?"

"Again, no idea." Mum patted the cardboard box. "There's no return address, and the delivery man didn't know, either."

Sirius stood there, staring at it. "I wonder what's inside," he whispered.

Mum laughed. "Well, if you open it, you might find out!"

With Mum's help, Sirius tipped the box onto its side, then cut away the tape that was holding it shut. He peered inside and saw … plastic bubble wrap. Lots and lots of bubble wrap. He pulled out the top layer, but the rest of it was wrapped around whatever was inside. He managed to slide the first mysterious object out and unwrap it, being careful because it was so heavy.

It was a metal dish, about the size of the serving platter Mum used when they had guests for dinner. The front was smooth and gently curved in the centre. Four metal rods were positioned along the outside edge of the dish and met in the middle, connected to what looked a bit like a microphone. There was a metal box with wires attached to the back.

Sirius studied the object. It looked familiar. Could it really be what he thought it was?

"It looks like a satellite dish," suggested Mum.

"No," whispered Sirius, "I don't think it is."

Excitedly, he reached back into the box to pull out more bubble-wrapped parts, including wires, more rods, some screws and a tripod. The final piece of bubble wrap contained a laptop computer.

"Oh, my goodness!" said Mum.

"It's a radio telescope." Sirius's voice was full of awe. "My own radio telescope!"

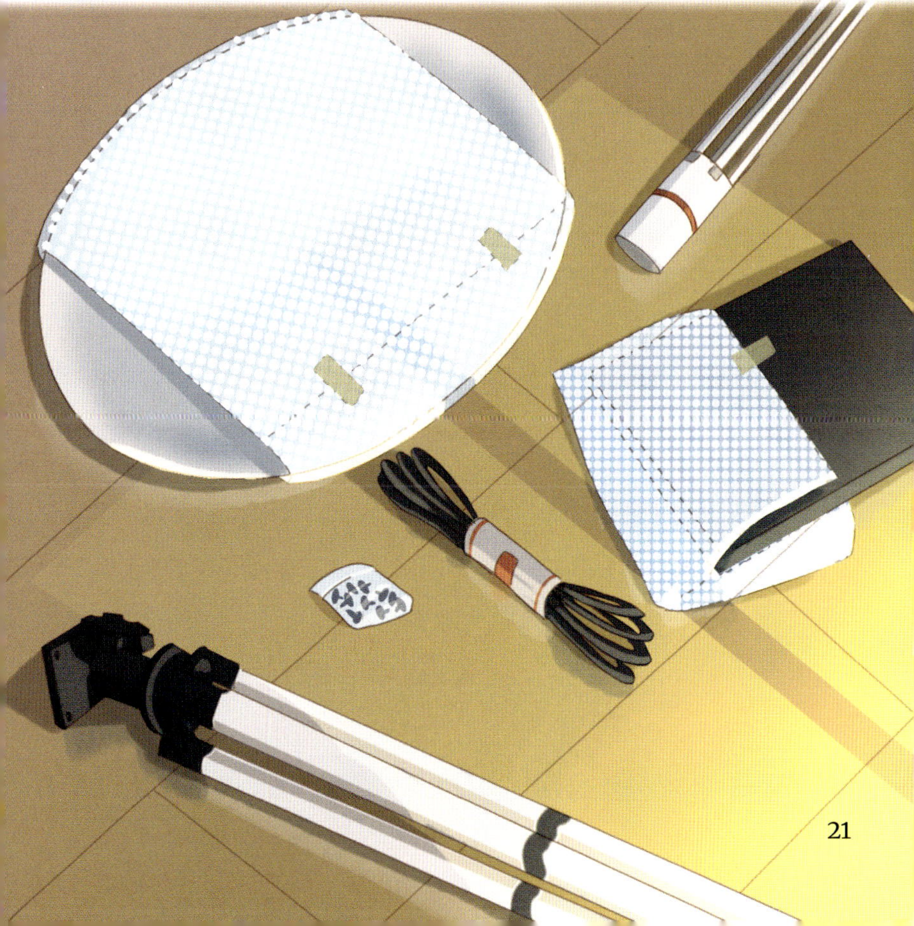

Sirius knew all about radio telescopes. After all, his dad was working with one of the largest ones in the world, which would be about two hundred times bigger than this one.

When most people heard the word “telescope”, they thought about optical telescopes. Optical telescopes used glass lenses and mirrors to focus light, allowing a person to see faraway objects. But radio telescopes used a dish to capture radio waves that were passing through the air. These radio waves could then be used to form an image of something that was far away – even as far as outer space. Sirius always thought of it as listening to the universe.

“Do you think this is from Dad?” asked Sirius.

“Well, I suppose it could be,” said Mum uncertainly. “But if your dad sent it, why doesn’t it have any overseas postage stickers? And why didn’t he include a letter or a card?”

If it wasn't from Dad, thought Sirius, who could have sent it?

It was a mystery – a mystery that needed to be solved.

"I'm going to put the telescope together right now!" announced Sirius.

Chapter 5

Messages from Space?

There were instructions on the laptop for how to put the radio telescope together. There was also a special program on the laptop that ran the telescope. But there were no clues as to who might have sent it.

It took Sirius all afternoon and all evening to put it together. He started out with much enthusiasm, thinking that he would be able to listen to the universe, just like his dad was doing. But when his mum came to tell him that his dad wasn't able to speak to him that night, his excitement drained away. All he could think about was that his dad wasn't there.

So, when Sirius finally finished putting the radio telescope together and turned it on, he didn't take it outside to try it out. He left it sitting by the window … and he went to bed.

He dreamt about Dad. In the dream, Dad was off in the distance. Sirius was running towards him, but no matter how fast or how far he ran, Dad seemed to be getting further away.

Then, a strange sound broke into his dream – a whooshing, buzzing, crackling sound.

Sirius's eyes snapped open. He was still in bed, but he wasn't dreaming the sound. It was real. And it was coming from the radio telescope by the window. He must have forgotten to switch it off before going to bed.

Sirius sat up and listened. He thought it sounded like electronic wind. But there was more to it – there were muffled beeping sounds in the background, like Morse code or something similar. Could it be a message of some sort?

Sirius jumped out of bed and rushed to the telescope. But the sound had already faded away.

Chapter 6

Sounds from Sirius

Sirius spent the next day at school distracted by thoughts of the sounds he had heard coming from the radio telescope.

Was it a dream? he wondered. *Surely not. It must have been real.*

Even so, he didn't feel ready to share it with anyone. Not until he was sure he knew what the sounds were.

Sirius hadn't checked the laptop last night. Despite being woken by the sounds, he had been so sleepy that he was unable to think straight. After the sounds had faded away, he had gone right back to sleep.

So, as soon as Sirius got home from school, he headed straight for his room and the radio telescope. The laptop hadn't recorded the sounds from last night, but the software did show where they had come from in the night sky. The dish had been pointed at Sirius, the star he was named after!

Sirius could barely contain his excitement. His star! The radio signals had come from his star!

"Mum! Mum!" he called out.

His mum came running into his room. "What? What is it?"

He told Mum what he had discovered. "I can't wait to tell Dad about it," he finished.

"Oh, I'm sorry, honey," said Mum. "Your dad can't make a video call tonight. He's busy with something on the project and can't call until Friday."

"Again?" Sirius felt the excitement drain out of him in an instant. Dad was supposed to talk to him every night. And Sirius had been so eager to ask Dad if the radio telescope was from him.

"How about we set up the radio telescope outside tonight?" suggested Mum. "See if you can pick up the signal again."

"I don't know."

"What? Are you *serious*, Sirius?" Mum giggled at the old joke. It was something Dad said all the time. "You should get as much data as you can between now and Friday," Mum continued. "Then you can give your dad a full report."

Sirius perked up. "Maybe."

"No maybes," insisted Mum. "Let's do this."

Mum helped him move the equipment outside after dinner, setting it up on the deck. Sirius connected the laptop, started the software and watched as the dish moved to point towards the brightest star in the night sky.

Mum put a blanket and a pillow onto the deck chair, and Sirius made himself comfortable. He listened carefully for any sounds from the laptop, but there were no signals … no sounds at all.

At nine o'clock, Mum suggested that it might be time to go to bed. Sirius begged her to let him stay up longer.

"Okay," she agreed with a smile. "Just a little bit longer."

Mum brought him a mug of hot chocolate. He snuggled under the blanket with his warm drink and looked up at the night sky.

"I wonder what's out there," he whispered to himself.

Chapter 7

Aliens?

Eyes wide, Sirius watched the radio telescope. The dish had started to spin, and as it spun, a sound was coming through the laptop speakers.

It started off as garbled electronic noise. Then, it smoothed out into a high-pitched hum. In the background, so quiet that Sirius could barely hear it, was what sounded like a voice.

As the voice gradually got louder, Sirius could make out a word.

"Greetings!"

Had he heard that right? Had he imagined it?

"Greetings!" the voice repeated. "Greetings from Sirius! This is a message for planet Earth. We would like to tell you about our world."

He wasn't imagining it. Sirius couldn't believe his ears. It *was* aliens. Aliens from Sirius were sending him a message!

He rushed up out of the deck chair, but he got tangled in the blanket. He tripped and went crashing to the ground.

Sirius woke up with a start. He was still in the deck chair, wrapped up in the blanket. The empty mug was on the table beside him. He'd been dreaming. He must have fallen asleep while waiting for the radio telescope to pick something up.

Wait a minute, he thought. *It* is *picking something up*. The same sounds that had woken him last night had woken him again.

Sirius quickly turned to the laptop. The sounds were coming from the star Sirius again. This time, the computer was recording them.

Could these sounds be from aliens, he wondered, *just like in my dream?* Perhaps aliens had somehow sent Sirius the radio telescope so he could receive their messages.

He shook his head.

No … that's just silly, he thought.

Chapter 8

Presentation

"This is a photo of the radio telescope my dad is working with." Sirius pointed to the TV screen in the classroom. "It's in West Virginia, in the USA. It's the biggest fully steerable radio telescope in the world. It's on a rotating base, and it also has a tilting mechanism, so it can point to any part of the sky!"

He clicked through to the next screen. "And this is a photo of my own radio telescope. It's a lot smaller and nowhere near as powerful. But it can still pick up radio waves from space."

"It looks like your dad has taught you a lot about radio telescopes," said Ms Whitford. "Maybe you should explain to the class about radio waves."

"Yeah," called out Ava, one of the loudest students in his class. "Are there radio stations in space? Are they run by aliens? Do they play the latest alien songs?"

The class laughed.

“Radio waves are used by radio stations here on Earth,” explained Sirius. “Certain frequencies are used to carry voices and music, and we pick them up on our radios. Radio waves are actually a type of electromagnetic radiation, which is energy that is made by all sorts of things, like planets, stars and galaxies. All these things give off radio waves, and radio telescopes can pick them up.”

The class had quietened down. Even Ava was listening with interest.

Sirius clicked through to the next screen, which was a photo of the laptop connected to his radio telescope. "Now, this is the sound that I picked up on my radio telescope." He clicked on the sound file.

A humming noise filled the classroom as the students listened intently. It wasn't as dramatic as the alien message from Sirius's dream, but he thought it was even more exciting, because it was real.

Again, Sirius wondered if his dad had sent him the telescope. He couldn't wait to tell Dad about the mysterious noise.

Chapter 9

Surprises

"Sirius!" Mum's voice called from inside. It was after dinner, and Sirius was out on the back deck, hoping to pick up more radio waves. "Your dad's online!"

Sirius jumped up from the deck chair and raced inside to see Dad's smiling face on the computer screen.

"Dad, Dad, Dad!" Sirius could barely contain his excitement. "I've picked up radio signals from space. And they're from Sirius! And I've got a radio telescope! And it's really cool. And did you send it? And –"

"Whoa! Calm down, Star-boy," said his dad, laughing. "Take a breath."

Sirius plonked himself down onto the kitchen stool and inhaled slowly.

"Now," continued his dad, "I know all about the radio telescope. And I know about the radio waves."

"How do you know?" asked Sirius. "Did Mum tell you?"

"She didn't have to tell me," he said. "I know about it … because I arranged it!"

"You arranged for me to get signals from Sirius?"

"Well, yes, kind of," said his dad. "Just settle in for a moment, and I'll explain."

Sirius nodded eagerly.

"Before I left, I arranged for the radio telescope to be sent to you from the university where I worked. It's a bit better than your average home kit." He smiled. "I modified it before I left, and I set up the laptop. I programmed the software to home in on Sirius, because that's what I'm working on."

"Really?" Sirius almost jumped off the stool in excitement.

"Yes, really," continued his dad. "The project I'm involved with is monitoring those signals. I thought it would be cool if you could monitor the same signals. Of course, your set-up is nowhere near as powerful as what we have here at the Green Bank Observatory, but at least it's something."

"Cool!" Sirius was so overwhelmed, so excited, that he couldn't think of anything else to say. He and his dad were listening to the same star, even though they were in different parts of the world!

"But wait … there's more!" Dad paused and grinned at him.

Mum came to stand behind Sirius, putting a hand on his shoulder and smiling. "You're going to love this, kiddo."

"I know how much you're missing me," Dad began. "I'm missing you, too, Star-boy. So, your mum and I have talked things over, and we've organised something I think you'll like."

"What?" asked Sirius breathlessly. He couldn't imagine anything better than what Dad had already done.

"Well …" Dad said, still grinning. "How would you like to come to the USA to visit me and see the Green Bank Observatory?"

Sirius's eyes widened. His heart started pounding. He threw his arms in the air.

"YES!"

Chapter 10

Waiting

Sirius yawned. It was a week later, and he was out on the deck again.

He put down his empty mug of hot chocolate and picked up his notebook. He had decided to keep a radio telescope journal. He would write down all his observations and experiences with the radio telescope, and what signals it picked up. That way, when he visited Dad, he could give him a report.

Maybe they could even compare notes.

Sirius knew now that the sounds the radio telescope was picking up were not made by aliens. They were radio signals being given off by the star itself. *His* star. The signals would help his dad put together an image of the star and any planets that might be orbiting it. It was really exciting!

Sirius smiled to himself. Waiting was going to be tough. His trip to the USA was planned for the mid-year school holidays, which were still months away.

But that was okay. He was going to go see his dad. And that was all that mattered.